book **Very good**

This Ladybird Book belongs to:

Christine Zhang

DAMAGE NOTED

This Ladybird retelling
by
Nicola Baxter

Published by Ladybird Books Ltd
27 Wrights Lane London W8 5TZ
A Penguin Company
3 5 7 9 10 8 6 4 2

© LADYBIRD BOOKS LTD 1994

Printed in Italy

12/03
4.50

FAVOURITE TALES

The Enormous Turnip

illustrated
by
PETER STEVENSON

based on a traditional folk tale

One sunny morning a man decided to plant some turnip seeds.

He fetched his fork from the shed and dug a patch of his vegetable garden. It was hard work! He made sure that there were no weeds or big stones.

Then, very carefully, he sprinkled the tiny turnip seeds in a row.

The man took great care of his turnip seeds. Every day, as soon as he woke up, he went down to his vegetable garden and gave them some water.

In only a few days, little green leaves started to appear.

"These are going to be fine turnips," the man said to himself.

The turnips grew very quickly, as turnips do. But one turnip grew faster than all the rest.

Soon it was twice as big as the other turnips. The man was astonished.

"I can almost *see* it growing!" he said proudly.

But the turnip didn't stop. It grew bigger and bigger and bigger until it was… *ENORMOUS!*

One day the man decided that it
was time to pull up the enormous
turnip.

"We can have it for our dinner,"
he said to his wife. "I'm sure it
will taste as good as it looks!"

So the man took hold of the turnip's huge leaves with both hands and he *pulled*…

and he *pulled*…

and he *pulled* with all his might.

But he couldn't pull up the enormous turnip!

The man called to his wife. "I'm going to need some help with this turnip!" he laughed.

So the man *pulled* the turnip and the woman *pulled* the man. They *pulled* with all their might.

But they couldn't pull up the enormous turnip!

The woman called to a little boy.
"Can you come and help us with
this enormous turnip?"

So the man *pulled* the turnip and
the woman *pulled* the man and
the little boy *pulled* the woman.
They *pulled* with all their might.

But they couldn't pull up the
enormous turnip!

A little girl was walking past. "Please come and help us with this enormous turnip!" called the little boy.

So the man *pulled* the turnip and the woman *pulled* the man and the little boy *pulled* the woman and the little girl *pulled* the little boy. They *pulled* with all their might.

But they couldn't pull up the enormous turnip!

The little girl called to her dog.
"Here boy! Come and help us!"

So the man *pulled* the turnip and
the woman *pulled* the man and
the little boy *pulled* the woman
and the little girl *pulled* the little
boy and the dog *pulled* the little
girl. They *pulled* with all their
might.

But they couldn't pull up the
enormous turnip!

The dog saw a large orange cat walking along the fence. "Woof!" he said. "Come and help us!"

So the man *pulled* the turnip and the woman *pulled* the man and the little boy *pulled* the woman and the little girl *pulled* the little boy and the dog *pulled* the little girl and the cat *pulled* the dog. They *pulled* with all their might.

But they couldn't pull up the enormous turnip!

The cat spied a little mouse sitting under a cabbage leaf. "Miaow!" she called. "Come and help us!"

So the man *pulled* the turnip and the woman *pulled* the man and the little boy *pulled* the woman and the little girl *pulled* the little boy and the dog *pulled* the little girl and the cat *pulled* the dog and the little mouse *pulled* the cat.

They *pulled*…

　　and *pulled*…

　　　　with all their might.

"Don't… stop!" panted the man.
"I think… yes, I think… we've
done it!"

And at that the turnip came flying out of the ground. The cat fell on top of the little mouse and the dog fell on top of the cat and the little girl fell on top of the dog and the little boy fell on top of the little girl and the man fell on top of the woman and what fell on top of the man?

The most enormous turnip anyone had ever seen!

When everyone had finished laughing they picked themselves up.

"You must stay and have dinner with us," said the man and his wife to the little boy and the little girl and the dog and the cat and the little mouse.

The turnip was *DELICIOUS!* And you know, it was *so* enormous that they haven't finished eating it yet!